Stolen

THE PREQUEL

DANI RENÉ

Blurb

I never believed in evil.
I never thought the devil was real.
Until I was stolen.

***

I knew Satan existed.
I was convinced I'd be like him one day.
Until my heart was stolen.

Would she be the one to set me free?
Or will I be the one to steal her life?

*This is an extremely dark story with numerous triggers, please be warned. Due to scenes of an adult nature, this book is for 18 ONLY.

Do you follow me?

If you'd like to keep up to date on my new releases, sales, and all the news for future work, check out my social media links, or sign up for my newsletter and get a free, unpublished novella, exclusive to my newsletter subscribers!

Newsletter: https://goo.gl/xx3bbj

Website: www.danirene.com

Facebook: http://bit.ly/DaniFBPage

Twitter: http://bit.ly/DaniTwitter

Instagram: http://bit.ly/DaniIG

BookBub: http://bit.ly/DaniBookBub

Goodreads: http://bit.ly/DaniGoodreads

Amazon: http://bit.ly/DaniAmazon

Dedication

This is for those who like to dive into the darker, twisted worlds, this one is for you.

Prologue
DRAKE

THERE ARE ONLY SO MANY DEAD BODIES you have to bury before your life becomes nothing more than a long-winded repeat.

Over and over.

Again and again.

The blood is the same.

The graves are the same.

I smile when I do it now. When I dig a six-foot hole, I revel in the harsh stench of bodies — rotting and vile. It's a reminder I'm a Savage. I was born into this life, and I'll die in it.

The pieces of flesh and bone still chill me to my soul, but there isn't any salvation for me. My life has been tainted by the sins that come with the last name I've been born with.

I bear the sins of my father.

I carry the cross of his actions.

And one day, I'll be forced to run the organization he's built.

With each body I dig a grave for, and with every heart I've seen cease to beat, I know there's no escape. As much as I want to run, there are people here I can't leave.

Two boys.

My brother.

My best friend.

They'll forever have me here, living the life the man who's kept us prisoners for so long has forced us into.

A dark journey.

A sordid road.

And there is no escape.

Unless . . .

We're severed.

One
DRAKE

CLOSING MY EYES, I BREATHE IN THE STENCH of the dungeon. No matter how many years I've been here, I'm still affected by the smell of the filth my father keeps them in. Each cell — cold and desolate — empty except for a bed and a bucket. When I first came down here, I was shocked, angry, confused, but it's become normal.

We all have our crosses to bear. Mine comes in the form of a family name I'd rather never have been born with. Every day, I wish I'd died with my mother when she birthed my brother and me.

My job is simple though. In this hell, I'm the one who gets them ready for the horror that lies ahead of them. I take those pretty, stolen toys who are thrown into the cells and I make sure they know there aren't any cuddles and sweet words. I'm the asshole parents warn you about.

Pulling on my suit jacket, I take a look in the mirror hanging against the gray wall in the dank office. This room is dimly lit for one reason — it's where the cameras are set up. Where we watch them. My dark hair is disheveled as usual, the blue in my eyes a stark contrast to my tanned skin. Most of my father's female clients want to fuck me. The men want to bend me over and make me grunt their names and beg them to hurt me, but that's never going to happen. I don't do shit with clients.

I do, however, get to touch the pretty toys we get in here. If they're listed as virgins, I don't go near them; but those who aren't, they're fair game. A good, hard fuck eases the tension for a little while.

No love.

No affection.

Just pleasure.

It's who I've become, and I'm proud of it. I've been

told before I'm a bastard, and I wear that label with pride. It's easy to turn off the switch. There's nothing left inside me; there is only death in my eyes. I've perfected the icy glare that has every girl cowering when I stalk into her cell.

I'm broken.

I'm off limits.

I'm Drake Savage.

And like the name says, I am a savage. I'll fuck you up so bad nobody will recognize you — physically or emotionally. My favorite though is mentally. Fucking with someone's mind is my forte. It's the one thing I strive to do well. Needling my way in, into the depths where you hide your fears. That's where you'll find me. And that's where I'll lie until the moment you take your last breath.

The only people I allow close are my best friend, River, and my brother, Dante.

All cameras are on when I cast a quick glance at them. In an hour, Frederick will be here to watch them.

His thankless job is to make sure the toys don't kill themselves by doing something stupid, like bashing their skulls against the wall or some shit.

I head out to the long hallway leading to the kitchen. It's empty. I know it will be because nobody is up this early. Our home has become a wasteland to love and affection. When I used to walk into the rooms, I'd find traces of our babysitter, but she walked out when we turned twelve. There's nothing even close to warmth in this place. The old woman couldn't deal with my father and ran. She never looked back, and I don't blame her.

Even though she offered some semblance of motherly love, it didn't help. I was still tortured by what I'd witnessed. I broke long before the day she said goodbye to us. My father and his organization have different ideas about what kids are for, and I was shoved into the life long before I even knew what any of it meant.

I always tried to protect my brother from it, but before long, he was taught we can never have a normal life. We'd always be the broken boys. The darkness in our souls will eventually completely take over, and we'd be just like him.

Just like the monster who made us.

Just like Malcolm Savage.

Two
CAIA

I SHIFT.

I can't move without my muscles protesting. They're angry and rabid.

There's a burning sensation that seems to be coursing through my veins, in every part of me. I feel as if I'm on fire. But when I'm still, the scorching heat isn't there. So, I lie there, my eyes closed. Heavy from something I'd been given, I can only guess.

I can't recall what happened. My head is filled with a foggy reel of blurry images. I can't pick them apart, and n't remember where I was or even who was there. I think it was a birthday party. The girls from school, those whom I called my friends, told me to go along for the ride. And I did. For the first time in my life, I broke my father's rules. They weren't really friends, but they were the popular girls, and I wanted to experience what it was like in their world.

Being the daughter of a well-known multi-billionaire, I've always been kept within the confines of my father's rules and regulations. His face is always plastered in the newspapers. His name is mentioned online more times than I can count.

I'm meant to keep myself on the straight and narrow. Nobody would know I've smoked a joint. And I enjoyed it. No one would ever guess I've kissed a boy. And tonight — at least, I think it's tonight — I was meant to have sex.

My first time.

There's an icy ache in my limbs causing tears to sting behind my lids. I don't know where I am, but when I finally crack my eyes open, I can't see anything in front of me, only darkness. There aren't even shadows to promise me a sliver of light in the space I'm in. Perhaps I'm locked in a box.

My fingertips trail along my arm, and I feel blood — at least, what I would guess is blood — dried and cracked on my skin. When I woke up moments ago, the cold was so harsh it caused my teeth to chatter loudly. I try to move again, to roll over, but it's pointless.

My body is rigid, almost paralyzed.

It's cold. Bitterly cold. It's as if I've been left in a freezer without any clothes or blankets to stifle the temperature. My arms prickle, as if a thousand pins are being shot into my flesh at resounding speed. I blink. The tears that burn my eyes dry before they reach my ears. I'm on my back, looking up into blackness so thick it threatens to choke me.

A click echoes in my ears like a foghorn warning a passing ship. A clank. The scrape of steel on the cement floor, or what I'm guessing is concrete.

"There she is." A deep rumble comes from somewhere in the darkness. I expect my visitor to say something more, but he doesn't. Silence falls around me again, enveloping me in its stifling madness. No words, not even a scuff of a shoe. Another switch clicks, and I'm bathed in a faded-yellow, luminescent glow.

"Wh-what am I do-doing here?" I croak, my throat protesting at the measly utterance. Five whole words voiced from my lips, and they sound like sandpaper grating against wood.

Raspy. Harsh.

I blink. Once. Twice. When my vision finally clears, I'm met with the steel-gray glare of a man I've never seen before. He's older, far older than I am at my eighteen years. He may even be as old as my father. His hair is silver, matching his cold eyes. There's a dusting of stubble on his face. It's dark, yet there's gray streaks through it as well, hinting that he must be in his early forties, perhaps even older.

He has a smirk on his face, evil, almost devilish. When he leans in closer, I try to make out who he is, but he's a stranger to me. The corner of his mouth kicks up; a sneer curls his vile mouth. He looks satisfied that he has a girl, a young girl, tied up in a dungeon.

What will he do to me?

I can't think about that right now. The only thing I need to focus on is the asshole before me.

"Your daddy sure does love you, poppet," he whispers across my skin, causing goosebumps to dot my bare flesh. The deep baritone of his voice vibrates through me, reminding me he's in charge. He doesn't need to tell me; it's clear in his expression.

I shiver, both from the cold and his ferocious stare. He looks angry, but there's another emotion brewing in his stormy eyes.

Lust.

"What?" I croak once more, only to earn myself a chuckle so deep and rumbling it sounds like thunder rolling in.

"He wanted me to pay him five million for you," the stranger informs me. "But I believe you're worth so much more than that." This time, he coos.

His hand reaches for me, his knuckles trailing a white-hot path down my icy cheek. The warmth of his skin against my almost-frozen flesh is a welcome comfort, and I find myself leaning into his touch.

"That's it, sweetheart," he whispers in a husky tone. "I'll be your daddy now."

"No, no," I whimper, pulling away from him, but he's too fast. Thick, calloused fingers grip my face harshly, turning my head to face him. His eyes glow with feral rage. His voice may have been the thunder, but his actions are the storm. He forces me to look at him, and I know there's no way I can fight the blizzard of this man. I'm ready for the lashing of lightning to burn me alive.

"Listen to me," he commands with fury burning through his words, igniting fear within my very core. "I don't care if you say no. In fact, I want you to say no. When you fight and wriggle against me, I'll fuck you harder. I'll make you fucking bleed all over me, all over my cock, and when I'm done, I'll ensure you clean me with your pretty pink tongue." His laugh is manic, vibrating off the walls as it tumbles from his slim, red lips.

"Sir." A voice at the door draws his attention. "We

have contact," the man says. When my captor moves, I get a glimpse of the stranger at the exit to the hell I'm locked in. His eyes land on me for a split second before averting his gaze to his boss.

"And they know what we have?" my captor questions. The answer is a nod. "Good. Get her ready."

The stranger walks into the room. He has a confident stride, as if this is the most natural thing for him to do. His body is large, foreboding, with broad shoulders and a tapered waist. I take him in, wondering if I could fight my way free. If I can get my hands on a weapon, I'll be able to do something other than lie here like a fucking toy.

The dress shirt he's wearing is a dark color, but not black. Perhaps charcoal. His slacks match, but his boots are black leather with worn cracks. He doesn't speak, but I take my time watching him move around the room.

He fills a bucket from the sink in the corner, the sound of water causing my bladder to ache.

"I need . . ." When I utter the words, he spins on

his heel to pin me with a glare. "I, uhm, need to pee," I tell him as embarrassment flushes through me, heating my cheeks, traveling down to my chest.

"Piss yourself on the mattress. The next girl won't be here till it's dry."

My mouth falls open, gaping at him in shock. Horrified at having to do what he said. I turn away, attempting to not listen to the trickle of the tap.

"Don't mind me, doll, I've seen much worse." This time he chuckles. "Working with him, I've cleaned piss, blood, and shit when he's finished with one of you, so you're definitely not special," he continues, not looking my way.

He picks up the bucket and strolls over to the icy metal bed I'm bound to. My wrists ache. Pins and needles pierce me as I tug and pull to get free, even though I know it's a pointless exercise. Standing above me, he takes the bucket and tips it over me and the mattress I'm lying on.

A squeal of surprise is wrenched from me, bouncing off the walls. I tug on my restraints only to have the twine bite into my torn skin, and I feel the trickle of water and blood as it oozes its way over my flesh.

The cold has nothing on what I feel now. My body is frozen. My limbs lose all feeling, and my teeth chatter loudly against each other.

My tormentor captures me in his arms, and I realize he's unbound me from the headboard. Even though I'm loose, I'm free, I'm still bound in another way. I'm so cold I can't move but then he's lifting me. My arms flail, one at my side and the other on my lap.

He turns us to leave the cell I've been in, but as he squeezes me through the doorway, my stomach lurches, and my bladder releases warm liquid over his stomach and arms.

"Are you fucking pissing on me?" he shouts, dropping me on the cold concrete floor. I land with a harsh thud on my hip, which causes me to cry out in agony. I grab at the side of my body, attempting to ease the pain shooting through me, to no avail.

His hands swipe at his shirt and slacks, but they're

drenched in my urine.

"You little bitch!" His foot makes contact with my stomach with a resounding thud. My lungs lose all air. My hands fly to my abdomen in an attempt to protect myself, but I know it's futile.

"Stop playing with the toys," the captor's voice comes from behind me. My vision is blurry, but I can make out the man who has just knocked the breath from my lungs.

He leans in, his face close to mine in a sneer so cold it turns my blood to ice. "I'll make you pay, little toy. That silky hair is like the wings of a bird, and I'll pull and tug until you have nothing left. And then, you'll fly no more," he grits out angrily.

Before he turns to leave, he spits on my face, saliva splattering on my cheek.

"Enough!" my captor orders him. "She's worth more alive and looked after."

Then I'm being tugged to my feet, dragged and thrown into a room which resembles a horror movie bathroom. Blood pools on the floor, the walls have the word help painted in the crimson liquid, and my stomach turns when I think about what happened.

"Clean yourself. Clothes will be set out for you when you're done."

The older man turns, leaving me in the room with no privacy as the door is no longer on its hinges.

I open the tap, cupping my hands and splashing the frigid water on my face. The toilet sitting to my right is stained with black marks, which makes my stomach roll.

I shove my panties down, hovering over the seat. Once I'm done, I wipe myself with the hard paper used for cleaning kitchen counters. The scrape of it against my sensitive flesh only makes the torture worse. My skin is normally sensitive to abrasions, and I can only imagine it's bright red from the burn over my core.

As I head out of the bathroom, I look around, praying I find a doorway, an exit, but as I feel along the dark wall, I find nothing.

I'm a prisoner, and there's nothing I can do about it. Sighing, I give up after my third attempt at trailing my fingers over cold, smooth concrete.

Making my way back toward the room, I find a white, cotton dress on the bed, noting the mattress is no longer on the metal frame. He must've moved it since he decided to soak me, along with the thin mattress, in water. I pick up the dress; the feel of the fabric is soft between my fingers. It's pretty, but far too big for me. I slip it on, thankful for the chance to cover my modesty. Not that it will help. I'm sure the men have already seen me naked while I was passed out.

I sit on the bed frame and wait. My tormentor, whom I earlier relieved myself on, arrives once more with a look that tells me not to try anything. He stalks closer, and I notice he's dressed immaculately. The suit he's wearing hugs every muscle of his lean frame. He's tall, probably over six feet. There's dips and valleys in the shirt, and I realize he must be extremely toned to look that good in a suit. My eyes drop to the front of his pants, finding a hard bulge against his zipper. It's so close it catches my eye.

"You look pretty all cleaned up," he smirks, causing my gaze to lift back to his.

His mouth tilts into a smile, which causes me to catch my breath. He's handsome. Devilishly so. His square jaw is smooth. The dimples dipping on either cheek are deep, making him look far younger than I think he is. He turns to the sink in the room again, ignoring me as he fills the bucket, and I wonder if he's going to drench me again.

"Why do you do this?" I question, suddenly anxious to see if he has any human emotions left from working down here. I don't know where my confidence comes from, but I want to stifle it back down when he turns to regard me with a penetrating blue glare. The color of his irises is almost see-through, reminding me of sunshine streaming through a window on a bright morning. Sadness washes over me when I realize I may not see the sunshine again. There's tension in the air, reminding me of when my father would tell me I shouldn't do things or he'd admonish me for wanting to go out with a boy.

"If you ask questions, you'll not make it through the night," he warns, his gaze piercing me. It's so harsh I'm bruised by the mere look he offers.

His words are a cold reminder he's not my friend and I shouldn't think he's here to save me. He isn't. He's as much of a monster as the man who wants to hurt me.

He leaves the bucket on the floor of my room and pulls me up by my arm. Then, he shoves me in front of him and warns, "Behave, and you'll get out alive."

I don't ask what he means. I don't even look away from the path in front of me. Instead, I focus on each step I take. We silently make our way down a long, dark hallway.

At one point, he maneuvers his way in front of me to open a door. My eyes adjust to the darkness, but my tormentor is hidden in the shadows. His dark suit makes it difficult for me to see him, and when he comes to a stop, I slam into his solid back.

Muscles tighten and tense when I place my hands on his shoulders. Every inch of him taut with . . . *Frustration? Anger?*

"Get your hands off me," he barks angrily, causing me to stumble backward.

"I . . . I'm sorry," I mumble, dropping my gaze to the floor, but he can't see me because the space we're standing in is pitch black. It's then a beep echoes around us, dinging loudly as a hiss of a door that's been locked for some reason slides open.

Light streams from the entry, and music comes from the other side. There's laughter traveling from where the muted yellow light is beckoning — men's chuckling, which sets me on edge.

My tormentor hands me an object in the darkness, then leans in closer. "This is the only option you have. Use it, don't use it. That's all up to you," he informs me.

When I turn to look at him, he's gone.

Straightening my shoulders, I step through the doorway and gasp.

Three
DRAKE

S<small>HOVING MY BEDROOM DOOR OPEN,</small> I <small>ENTER,</small> sighing when I see River on my bed. He's lounging against the headboard, his body naked except for the small pair of blue boxer-briefs hugging his hips and thighs. My bedroom is stark, just like me. The dark space, with the white and silver paintings along the walls are almost clinical. I don't like color. I don't enjoy being outside. The sun is far too cheerful for me to endure. Thankfully with my natural tanned skin I don't look like the walking dead.

His green gaze lifts to my blue one. Silence is heavy in the air as I shrug off my jacket. The clink of my gold, engraved cufflinks are the only sound when I drop them on my chest of drawers. Next are my slacks, then my shirt. When I'm in much the same attire as he is, I join him on the mattress.

"How is she?" he asks, knowing I've been in that hell all day. I want to tell him about her, about the feisty little girl.

"Malcolm isn't going to be happy about her," I inform him. "She's far too fiery, and she's not going to break easily." My assumptions on Caia are strong. I've never seen such fight in a girl before.

"Perhaps she'll be easier to break," he suggests, pulling me closer, and I place my head on his chest. His heartbeat slowly thrums in my ear. It's the only time I allow myself to not think about the dark. River is as broken as I am, and he understands there are times I just want silence.

"Dante is out with a girl," he informs me, and I hear the agony in his tone. River and my brother have history. I have a feeling my best friend is in love with my brother, but he's never said anything to me. Perhaps it's because I fuck River as well.

"Good for him," I respond, placing my hand on his soft cock, hoping to wake it up and have him forget Dante for a moment.

"You can't do that, you know," River smirks. I hear it in his words.

I don't look up at him, but question, "What?"

"Fuck me to make me think about you instead." Pulling my hand from his bulge, I sigh and push off the bed. Padding barefoot into the adjoining bathroom, I turn the shower on and shove my boxers down.

Under the spray, I close my eyes and imagine Caia. Her slim body, those big eyes filled with fight and innocence. I want to steal it. To fucking take everything from her so my father can't.

My cock jolts when I remind myself of her slight frame in my arms. She was so delicate, so fucking soft. Fisting my dick, I stroke it slowly, taunting myself with images of her, of what I could do to her.

I've fucked so many women in my short life, but there's something about tearing apart her body that does things to me. A fire burns in my veins when I squeeze my shaft, almost to the point of pain.

Realization dawns that I want to take her sweetness, and it stills me for a moment, but only one moment, because soon I'm pumping my release down the drain imagining her virtue slick on my cock.

I will have her.

I'll break her, make her mine, before she's taken and defiled worse than I ever can do to her.

The darkness surrounds me.

It always has. By the time I was thirteen, I had seen far too many horrors. But it's all him. He took and took, and when there wasn't anything left, he preyed on others. Then again, he's always done that. I recall the first time I learned what he was.

A monster.

It was that day my life changed. I'd never be the same again, and now that I'm twenty-five, I feel as if I'm an old, ragged man. Even though I'm only starting my life. Not the life I wanted, but the one I was thrust into at an early age.

There's a stench in the basement when I enter. Five rooms sit to my left, and another five to my right. That's ten captives he holds each year. One month, four weeks, he takes one of those lucky ten and ensures they shatter. The process is simple. They come in, they get tortured and used, and then on their final day, a group of men and women walk in, watch the show, and choose which they'd prefer.

He's broken them in for years. It's the way he gets off. I've seen the vilest of acts being done to girls over the years. He's had boys here too. However, they don't earn him enough, so he focuses on girls. They can offer him what boys can't.

And as many years as I've been here, I'm still trying to find a way out. A way where I can run with my brother and my best friend and never look back. Slowly, with each night that falls, I know that day will never come. But I hold onto that faraway emotion we're taught as kids.

Hope.

The problem is, in this place, that's a fruitless wish. There's no such thing as hope in here. Life will end here the same way it started. In agony. It's the cries and screams that haunt the walls of the mansion. Even though the captives are kept in the basement, being on the upper levels, even in my bedroom, I hear them. As if they echo to me, to taint me for what I've helped be done to them.

I recall the day I walked into the basement when he was in one of his *sessions*.

The door is ajar. There's a dim light telling me to run, to hide, but I don't. I'm intrigued. I'm ten years old, and all I want is to learn to be a good boy. He tells me I need to be, but I never understand what he means.

I reach the last, cold, concrete step and peek through the space in the door. A gold light comes from within. A scream so loud, so filled with pain I can't help stumbling back. It's a girl. I can tell that already.

I lean forward once more, and the door slides open another inch. The image before me causes me to retch. The sound echoes along with her screams, and he snaps his vicious glare at me.

"Bring him in." The familiar, deep voice I've known all my short life vibrates through the walls of the basement. Cold concrete greets my ass when I fall back.

Two strong meaty hands grip my bony shoulders, lifting me with no effort. My skinny legs flail wildly in the air as a man who's the size of an ogre carries me inside the room where he's standing.

"What the fuck is he doing in here?" the man questions.

I recoil when a hand reaches for my face. Gripping my neck, he lifts me onto a steel gurney and presses me flat on my back. The smell of blood is thick in the air, and I retch once more.

My body folds in the middle, my small arms hold onto my stomach, but he growls, ordering the ogre to bind my arms and legs to the four corners. Once I'm unable to move, he chuckles when I beg for mercy. But I know for a fact he won't *show it.*

The little girl on the gurney beside me is not moving. Her long blonde hair is matted with dark red liquid. It looks like she's sleeping —her eyes closed, her face at peace—and I notice her chest isn't moving. She's no longer breathing.

"What did you do?" My question is hoarse. My throat burns at the realization running through my mind. I shake my head when he looks at me and nods.

"She served her purpose." His words are cold, then I notice him pulling up his zipper on the dark slacks he always wears to work.

I don't understand. My brows crease in confusion. He hurt her. I know that.

"Perhaps we can have him trained?" the man asks the ogre. They both look at me as if I'm an experiment. I'm not sure what they mean, but my chest tightens, and my breathing gets more difficult.

"I think he'll be a good investment," the ogre agrees after a long while of studying me. He smirks, his mouth curling evilly as he watches me.

"Tie him in the training chair." The old man grins happily. He cups my cheek in his hand and leans in. His breath stinks of alcohol and blood which makes me choke on the spit dripping down my throat from his open mouth.

"What if he doesn't—?"

"I said tie him to the fucking chair," the man bites out angrily at the ogre. "He'll learn to appreciate my business. He is my son after all."

Shaking my head to clear it of the gloomy time in my life, I move into the empty cell and start my clean up. I couldn't sleep after I'd left her in that room, so here I am at one in the morning working when I should be asleep.

The wet mattress has already been pulled out of the room, and the bucket needs to be removed and cleaned. Grabbing the mop, I start on the floor now dried where she's pissed herself while I was holding her. I shouldn't have gotten angry, but it was her weakness I hated.

When he told me there would be more coming,

he mentioned bringing a new, special girl in. I knew what he'd want from me. I've become wary of the girls who arrive, because I know the moment I see them in their beauty, it will be the last time they'll ever look that way again. But after my jerk-off session last night, I closed my eyes, with River curled around me in bed, and saw her eyes. I recognized the plea in them. She needs a knight to save her, and as much as I never believed I could be anyone's savior, this girl makes me feel something I never did before — I want to be the one who saves her from the Devil himself even though it may kill me.

I want to sever the link to him and have her be mine.

But as much as I want that, I know I can't ever have her because he owns them all. Each one brought into hell, he takes them and makes sure they never see the light of day again.

But it's not the fact that he takes from them, it's the way he does it. A scrape of a boot sounds from behind me, and I find my brother at the door. He eyes me warily. We've both been working here for the man we call father for so long it's become second nature to clean up the mess left by each toy.

"She going to last?" he questions naturally, as if we're talking about the fucking weather. He looks like he's been well fucked, and I wonder who the girl was.

"I hope so." I've never uttered those words. Never once cared if the girls come back from their sessions or not, but with the pretty toy I've just led to the den, I wonder if I'll ever see those soulful eyes again.

"There's no hope in here, Drake," my brother grunts in frustration. He's younger than me by two minutes. But I was dragged into the darkness much earlier than he was.

"I know," I finally respond, causing him to glance at me. The blue eyes that match mine stare at me for a moment. My father told us we were a gift to him from our mother. That she had told him how special we were as she birthed us. In her screams, she told him we'd carry on the Savage legacy. I think he's full of shit.

My mother may be a stranger to me — I've only ever seen a handful of photos of her — but there's something in her gaze whenever she looked at the camera. A faraway look that reminds me of the girls in here.

Her ancestry took us back to Europe. Both our mother's and father's bloodlines originated there. But now we live in what is known as the "land of the free", which to me is a lie, because it seems to stifle everything good in our lives.

"Is she pretty?" he questions as he unscrews the bottle of bleach. The harsh scent still bothers my senses as he douses the floor in the clear liquid.

Is she?

Yes.

"It doesn't matter," I tell him, not answering his question because I know there isn't any reason for me to want her. As much as I could attempt saving her, it would be pointless.

"Then perhaps you should go in there and ask Dad

if he'll allow you to play the final round." I glance at my brother then. It's the first time we've really gotten to talk about something like this. An option of perhaps winning and keeping one of the girls.

But even so, if I do get her, she'll hate me for what I allow to happen to her. I've left her in there with the Devil himself. I know what she's going through right now. In my mind, I recall the *training chair*. My father's idea of teaching impressionable youths on the basics of human nature. That's a fucking joke. More like the intricacies of being an animal.

"That will never happen," I tell him.

"You never know," Dante murmurs as he carries the bucket from the cell and disappears, leaving me to wonder if I'll ever have a chance against our father.

Four
CAIA

MY TORMENTOR LEFT ME IN THE SOFTLY LIT room four hours ago with an object. It's small, and when I lift it to the light, I note it's a pocket knife. But the blade is serrated, and even though I've never been a fearful person, this makes me shudder. If I need this, then whatever I'm about to experience may kill me.

Nobody has come to me, but I'm locked in a small room where I can't see much. All I can hear is the melody from the other side. I've screamed, yelled for someone, but it's fallen on deaf ears. I have lost all sense of time, when suddenly the music and voices fade, hands grab me from behind and shove me into a dark closet.

The person wrenches the knife from my hand,

and in that moment, all hope leaves me. I'm blindfolded, and there are plugs in my ears to keep out the noise.

My body aches when I'm shoved forward and then forced to sit on a small wooden chair. My wrists and ankles are bound to the legs of the chair in seconds.

The person moves fast to ensure I can't fight, and then I'm left alone.

Seconds pass, then minutes.

"Please let me go. If you tell me why I'm here, I can get my father to talk to you. Do you want money? He has money." Nobody responds to my plea. Tears sting my eyes as my mind plays scenarios like a horror movie before me.

I'm hunched over. The tension in my shoulders is unbearable. I've tried tugging at the bindings, but they're knotted too tight. With each tug, the twine cuts into the harsh wounds from being bound to the bed earlier, and I know I'm not making it better by trying to pull myself free.

Suddenly, the plugs are pulled from my ears, and I

can hear the music again. Classical and operatic. It's not loud, merely a whisper, but almost torturous in volume.

"She's pretty," a deep rumble comes from somewhere. The blindfold hinders my sight, and I don't know how many people are in the room, but if I had to guess, I'd say two. The man who hurt me earlier and another. The stranger's voice is deeper, more ragged than my captor.

"Get her ready," a voice comes, the one of the men who's keeping me in here. "She's to be trained as soon as possible. I want her ready for next month's auction."

There are hands pulling at my arms and legs, untying me hastily from my bound position. Tugging my wrists together, he twines the rope tightly. Then suddenly I'm thrust into the air. A hard shoulder pressing into my stomach as he grips my ass and another arm snaking around my thighs.

He walks through the space I'm not allowed to see. When he finally sets me on my feet, I'm placed against a wall, or something cold and hard. Concrete. Perhaps the same type as the walls of the cell I woke up in.

My hands and legs are bound against the icy wall, and I'm once again locked in place with nowhere to go. A chuckle comes from my left, and his hot breath on my cheek causes me to shudder.

"Don't worry, pet, you'll soon enjoy this," he grits out in a devilish tone. His calloused finger paints something on my lips. As soon as my tongue darts out, the metallic flavor causes me to retch. "You look so pretty painted with crimson." His voice is cold as ice, and it chills me.

The blindfold is ripped from my face, and the harsh light is blinding for a moment. Blinking to clear the sting, I find myself in a small dark room and realize the blinding light is coming from the television set before me.

"What are you doing?" I croak, but he ignores me as he moves to the corner and pulls out a small trolley he wheels over to me. Placing it between my legs, I notice it has one of those magic wand vibrators attached to it. "Please, you don't have to do this." I know my words fall on deaf ears, but I try anyway.

He locks it in place and moves to the television shining a bright-white screen. When he clicks a remote, an image appears. It's a video paused on the title I'm sure is something gory from the word on screen.

Severed.

"Enjoy your movie night, princess." The man who reminds me of an evil ogre smirks viciously as he walks out, shutting the door with a resounding click. My gaze darts back to the screen, and before I can think about what's about to happen, the wand placed on my core starts a gentle vibration.

Another older man appears from behind me. He's dressed like a doctor, with blue plastic gloves and a stethoscope around his neck.

"We're going to test your restraint, little one," he smirks. "They asked for a strong one, a fighter."

I frown at this information, wondering who he's talking about, or even what he's talking about. "Please, why are you doing this?"

He doesn't respond, merely gestures to the screen with his chin, silently ordering me to turn my attention back to the television.

The name disappears, and a scene appears with a man who looks to be in his early forties, graying hair with a scraggly beard that reminds me of barbed wire. The lens follows him to a bed where a girl who can't be much older than my eighteen years is bound helpless.

I can't look away, and I can't close my eyes. I'm bound so well with my head fastened to hooks on the wall that don't allow me to move an inch. There's something on my eye lids that allow me to blink, but I can't keep them closed.

She's begging, crying, and pleading with him to let her go. The vibration between my legs intensifies, and I'm lost in pleasurable confusion. My body is reacting to the stimulation, but my mind recoils at the scene on the television.

I'm assaulted by the scene before me of the old man thrusting himself inside the girl. There are feral grunts, screams of pain, and when the lens zooms in, blood is dripping from where they're connected.

My body gives in to the pleasure. My stomach convulses from the scene before me. I can't stop my orgasm, and I can't stop the puke that's dripping from my chin. My mind feels almost fragmented, shattered and torn at the emotions racing through me.

The man, who's dressed in an immaculate suit, continues to violate her, to torture her with his cock, his grip around her neck tightens as her choking intensifies, while he spits on her. It's horrific to watch, and I'm afraid to see what's to follow. His large hand grips her tiny breast, tugging on the flesh harshly, as if he's trying to rip it off. Her cries echo in my ears, and his grunts fill the room.

It's sick.

It's vile.

And I can't move away, turn away from the scene. The large, silent man dressed in a white lab coat stalks closer, his hand holding an object dripping blood, and when I finally take a good look, I notice it's a human heart. At least, that's what I've seen pictures of in biology class. My body is rigid with fear, my blood turning icy cold. *What are they doing with that?* My thoughts are erratic, fliting between fear and revulsion.

"She had so many pretty parts," he sneers, pushing his hand holding the organ against my mouth as I try to fight him off. The screams still echo around me as he feeds me. With his other hand, I feel the pressure between my legs as he forces two thick fingers inside me. "You'll be broken soon, just like her."

I can't close my mouth as he shoves it into me, and I'm painted in the crimson liquid while the video plays, and my body leaps over an edge I've been fighting, but the assault on my clit is too much.

I'm drenched in red. My mouth and my shoulders are slick as he grips me, ensuring I'm soaked in the metallic liquid.

"So pretty, little girl," he sneers.

My body locks and convulses as pleasure shoots

through me. It's not from the scene. It's from the forced orgasm I've been subjected to. But the vibration only intensifies. I cry out, begging for mercy, even though I know they'll never offer it. I feel another release on the edge, it's right there, and the filthy words from the TV vibrate though me, and I cry out in pleasure, in pain, in disgust.

Another notch on the vibrator is turned up, and I'm wet. My clit is throbbing now, and I can't stop the moan that slips from my lips. A third orgasm is close, I'm watching a girl get violated, and all I can do is find release, pleasure watching pain.

The piece of filth steps back, admiring me shaking and shuddering wildly. My captor turns around and calls out to someone I can't see.

"Get Dante in here. She needs to be cleaned up."

"Why?" I whimper, attempting to spit the blood from my mouth.

He spins on his heel, glaring at me. "Because, little girl," he says in a low, menacing tone. "You're going to bring me a lot of money. Every part of you." His blue eyes glow with evil intent.

My body is rising to the edge. I'm standing on the precipice as the old man on screen pulls a blade from under the pillow and severs her head as the wand is turned to full pelt and I come harder than I've ever known a woman could.

My body is wracked with a sob, convulsions, and an orgasm that turns me inside out. My toes curl. I watch the head of a beautiful girl fall off the bed, and the man finds his own release in her now dead body.

When the door flies open, I'm crying. The white-coated man steps back after turning off the vibrator that's assaulted me for as long as the video had been repulsing me. He smirks at the newest member to the room.

"Get her cleaned up," he orders, then leaves us, his footfalls disappearing into the darkness.

The screen is black, but the dim light streaming in from the room beyond offers me a glimmer to see who's walked in. My tormentor. The dark-haired man with the blue eyes that remind me of an ocean. *Dante.*

"You're quite surprising," he tells me. "He'll make sure you break." It's a veiled threat, and I wonder if he's telling me that in warning, or if he's disgusted at what I've just been through.

"Help me."

He stills in his need to unchain me. "I'm not the good one, pet. Perhaps you're mistaking me for my brother. There's no escape from the dungeon. You either conform, or you die." *Brother?*

He continues to move swiftly, and then I'm in his arms, and I realize it's not my captor from earlier. He smells different. Not as spicy. He has a unique scent which I commit to memory. If there's two of them, perhaps I can figure out how to get them to help me.

When we enter the adjoining space, there's a bed he places me on. I'm shoved onto my stomach and once more bound to the metal poles on either end.

I'm open to him as he washes me, his fingers probing me painfully. I can't stifle the whimper and attempt to close my legs, but he only chuckles at the movement.

Once he's completed his task, he leans in close to my ear. "If you can survive this," he starts, "then perhaps there's hope for us all."

With that, I'm left alone to wonder what he means.

All I do know is that it can't be good.

Five
DRAKE

I HAVEN'T SEEN HER IN HOURS. MY MIND IS FILLED with images of what I imagine is going on inside that room. The cameras before me are empty. None of the girls who are in their cells have moved.

But Caia hasn't been returned to hers. I'm angry that she's captured my fucking attention so much, but I haven't been able to focus on anything else. Even River has been in here a few times to check if I'm still breathing. I don't think I am.

Shoving the chair along the concrete floor, I cringe at the noise it makes. The moment I rise, I see her cell door open and her body flung onto the mattress like a rag doll. Rage implodes through me, simmering in my veins like a goddamn poison.

What have you done to me?

I wait for the asshole to leave her cell before my feet hastily carry me to her door. As soon as it creaks, she opens her eyes wide and watches me. Her long, dark hair hangs matted to her head. I notice the blood that's been knotted in her locks, and my fingers itch to wash it out, to clean her, but I know if I go near her now, she'll scream. She'll lose her shit.

"Are you okay?" The question comes unbidden from my lips, causing me to cringe. Of course she's not okay.

"Does it look like I'm okay?" she bites back, causing me to chuckle. Jesus, she's beautiful when she's angry. Her pale flesh is marred with red welts, and I know she's been through phase one.

"Don't mistake my question for caring, little bird," I growl, stalking closer to her, causing her to cower in the corner. Her small frame shifting, offering me a glimpse of her white panties. She must've been changed before they brought her back in here, because those weren't what she

59

was wearing earlier.

"Fuck you," she mumbles, her wide eyes pinned on me as I lean over the bed. Reaching for her, I grip her hair. Fisting it harshly, I pull her closer toward me. A tremble trickles through her; goosebumps rise on her porcelain skin. She's perfection. Pure perfection.

"I'd be happy to oblige you, little raven," I smirk down at her.

Her lips purse into a tight line, and from the way her body is shaking, I'm certain she's a virgin. With a fierce tug, I pull her to the edge of the bed, her face against my groin.

"Feel that?" I whisper, a low hiss of a question that earns me a whimper, which only causes my dick to jolt against her cheek. "That's all yours if you want it," I tell her.

"Never."

I smile. I shouldn't be proud of her, I shouldn't even be hard for her, but something inside me has awakened, a beast that's hungry and wants a piece of the sweet fruit on the bed before me.

I lower my gaze to hers, finding her looking up at me. Her face has paled even more, making her eyes contrast against her flesh. Her lips are a soft, rosy color, and I wonder what they taste like. More so, I wonder how my cock would look sliding between them. Deep into her throat until she can't breathe. Until she's clawing at me, attempting to push me out.

"Your feisty little mouth is going to get you into trouble," I inform her, still holding onto her. Strangely, she allows me to keep hold of her hair. I wonder why she's not fighting.

"Just let me go," she says then. "I just want to leave, to go home." Her plea, along with that beautiful pout, is enough to have me shoving my zipper down. I reach for my cock and pull it from its confines.

"If you keep begging, I'm going to have to shut you up," I tell her, slapping her cheek with the thick angry shaft.

"You're disgusting," she bites out, and I'm done.

Pushing her to the bed, I grip her throat and press my fingers on either side, cutting off her air. Her tiny body flails wildly on the filthy mattress.

As soon as her lips open to attempt to pull in air, I shove my dick deep inside her pretty throat. It tightens, pulses, grips the bulbous head, and I'm lost in pleasure. Holding my dick in her body, I close my eyes, feeling her teeth scrape the base as she attempts to bite me.

Too bad the little princess will find out that I love the pain. It makes me even harder, throbbing inside her as I slowly pull out and slam back in. This time, the heat of her puke rises. Before she throws up, I pull out completely as she scrambles for the bucket.

Righting myself, I zip my slacks and watch her empty her stomach in the plastic bucket that's going to waft a stale stench all night. Her watery eyes meet my hard ones.

"You're worse than them," she tells me, stilling me for a moment before I reach for the bucket and head for the door. I don't respond, taking the filthy object to the cleaning room and grabbing a clean one.

Back in her cell, I set it down and turn for the door once more.

"You're broken, aren't you?"

Her question halts me at the door, my hand wrapped around the steel handle. Lowering my head, I cast a glance over my shoulder at her kneeling on the floor. She's shattered, her body still shivering as she regards me.

"I'm not broken, little bird," I tell her. "You'd have to be whole before you can break." I leave her alone to mull over my words before I go to my room for the night. I shouldn't have done what I did, but I couldn't help it.

In the shower, I recall how she felt. Just those few seconds of ecstasy and I've got my cock in my fist once more. As much as I fucked up, I don't regret a moment of it. If I could do it again, I would.

Six
CAIA

HE'S VIOLENT AND DANGEROUS. MY THROAT burns from his abuse, but my mind wonders how he's become so cold. When he looked at me, there was a flicker of affection, of something he refused to admit. His anger was palpable, a force that made him act out in a rage, but then guilt marred his handsome face.

He is handsome.

Far too beautiful to be in this place.

I've known what it's like to be hidden away. My father was overly protective of me, ensuring I'd never gone out partying like the other girls my age. I was like the princess locked away from the world, until the night I was stolen.

I stupidly went out of my way to defy my father for the first time in my life, and it's landed me in here. I lie back on the bed. In an attempt to close my eyes, I'm assaulted by the eyes of my captor. The man who looks so haunted it made me question him. I expected him to stalk toward me and slap me, or worse, but he merely glanced my way with such sadness it tugged my heart.

Stupid girl.

There's no way he can be good. He works for the devil, but he looks like an angel. My thoughts are at war. I can't shake the questions racing through my mind. I want to ask him everything. I want to delve into his mind and find out what he's hiding. But something tells me climbing those high walls he's built will be pointless.

He could be my way out of here. I should've asked him about his brother. Or even perhaps why they do this, what the point is of hurting people. No, not people, girls.

My chest aches, but the pain between my legs is like nothing compared to anything I've ever felt. Rolling over, I curl into a ball and hug my thighs to my chest. It's the only way I have some relief, but even then, there's no escape from the nightmares I know will follow. My eyes flutter, and I sadly allow sleep to steal me.

* * *

The creak of the door, the echo of metal upon the concrete wakes me. My body is still curled into a ball. When I move, every muscle tightens.

"Wake up."

The voice isn't that of my captor, and my heart sinks. It's not even his brother. When I finally manage to turn around, I find green eyes peering at me. It's my captor's friend. I'm not sure what his name is, but they both came to me on my first day here.

"You're going with me today." He smiles. It's a friendly gesture, but a cold pit of dread sits in my stomach at his words.

"Where . . . where am I going?"

"Today you're going to see what Drake can do," he informs me. That must be my captor. It would make sense if he and Dante are brothers, twins. Dante warned me last night he was the bad one, the violent one. I can only pray Drake is not as volatile.

"And Drake is Dante's brother?" He nods. "So, where is Drake taking me today?"

He stares at me for a moment, as if he's trying to figure out if he should tell me what's going to happen or not. I can't deny the fear trickling through my veins. Those green eyes hold far too many secrets as they linger on me.

"Drake is the second in command. Dante, third." He sighs, pulling a long white dress from the bag he'd been holding when he entered.

"And you?"

"I'm the foot soldier, sweet thing," he smirks. I notice then how handsome he is. When he's serious, those tattoos snaking up his neck from the white collar of his shirt make him look scary. But it's his dimpled smile that makes him seem less intimidating.

"You're only their lackey? Seems a bit strange. You and Drake looked like friends," I observe, causing him to stop at the foot end of the bed. He doesn't respond, merely throws the dress on the mattress.

"Get up, you'll need a shower before you go out there. I'll bring you something to wear as well." His gaze takes me in, sizing me up in the dirty clothes I'm wearing. "Tonight, you need to look perfect."

I silently take the material and slide it over my half-naked frame. The slight warmth it offers is welcome, but I know it won't last long. Comfort in this place is short-lived.

"I'll bring you food, and then I'll take you to him."

The man turns to leave, but I call to him, "What's your name, foot soldier?"

He drags his gaze over to me slowly, pinning me with a curious stare, and I'm certain he won't offer me his name. But then he smiles. "My name is River."

"I like that." I grin in return, and for the first time since I've been in here, I find light within the darkness.

"Don't mistake my smile for friendship, sweet thing," he says, twisting the handle on the door. "I'm not one of the nice men. Actually, this place doesn't have anyone nice you can befriend. It's best you don't become attached," he sighs. "Especially to Drake."

He leaves me wondering what he meant. How can I become attached to a man I don't know? A man who's most likely going to hurt me? Make me cry? Is that how he likes it? How he gets off?

I sit in silence and wait for my food to arrive, but even though River has given me a few answers, it's only unlocked so many more questions than I had before.

Seven
DRAKE

THE ROOM I'M IN IS LIT WITH CANDLELIGHT. I'm always reminded of the first time I was brought here. The nightmares that followed have never left me. Even though it's been years, I still see the images in my mind. They're ingrained behind my lids, and I know I'll forever be scarred.

But today, I have a job to do. The beast that resides within me is hungry. It's been a while since my father has allowed me to sate it. I'm looking forward to this pretty toy to feast on.

Closing my eyes, I take a deep breath. The gentle scent of lavender and eucalyptus hangs in the air. It's meant to be calming, but nothing about what I'm about to do will calm the beautiful Caia.

The tumbler sitting on the glass table is half filled with amber liquid that glimmers in the flames. I needed time to prepare, and now that she's on her way with River, I feel as if it's my first time.

I turn on the stereo. "Silence" by Beethoven greets me through the speakers, and I close my eyes to the melody of the piano. So ironic that soon there'll be no silence in this room.

The beast inside me roars to life when the door clicks open and I inhale her. The scent of this girl lingers as she enters and exits a space. There are many vices in my life that I allow to rule over me, but this need for her, it's something I can't contain for too much longer.

I turn to her. She's dressed in the white dress I asked River to give her. Purity. So fucking innocent. Too bad I want to tear her apart with my teeth. I hunger to drench that material in crimson.

I lift the tumbler to my lips, tipping my head toward my best friend who looks at me with sadness, knowing what I have to do. He leaves. We're alone then,

Caia and me. She glances my way, unsure, nervous, yet there's a flicker of indignation in her pretty eyes.

She offers a smile, which shoves me off kilter for a second before I right my stance and set the glass on the counter behind me.

"Sit." I gesture at the chair positioned perfectly where I need it. Silently, she obeys me, and I can't help smiling. *Such a good girl.*

Her hands are splayed on her thighs, her legs pinched together, and her long, dark hair hangs down her back in a sleek braid. River always ensures the toys are perfectly made up for me.

There isn't an ounce of make-up on her face, and I'm happy for that. I hate those fucking dolls that look fake when they're crying as I use them. Father was adamant that she's to remain a virgin. He told me to see if I can shatter her defiance, and I know that anything I do to her in here will not do that. She's far too strong. But I'll gladly give it a good try.

Her gaze finds mine. There's a plea in those wide

eyes. *No, darling, tonight, you'll not shock me like you did last night.*

"Why am I here?" she finally questions. I find that most times, if you leave them in silence for long enough, they'll break.

"You're here to learn, little bird," I tell her. Unbuttoning my suit coat, I shrug it off. Feeling her gaze roam over me, I turn and set the jacket on the chair. When I face her, she's staring at me, her lips slightly parted.

"And is my learning meant to make this ordeal easier?"

I consider her question for a moment. *Would it?* Perhaps. Stalking toward the bar, I grab the Scotch along with a small glass, which I fill to the brim. I set the drink before her on the table and straighten.

"Drink that," I command, watching her eyes narrow with suspicion. *Fuck.* This girl is utterly intoxicating, more so than the alcohol I've consumed.

"I'm eighteen."

"I don't give a fuck. I said drink it," I bite out, my

teeth clenched so tight it feels as if I'm about to crack them.

The song changes, and we're met with the melodic sounds of Lucas King, classic, dark, and haunting. Caia lifts the glass, sniffing the contents before scrunching up her nose in disgust.

"I don't have all day."

She glares at me but swallows the shot in one grimacing gulp. When she sets the glass down, she sits back once more, waiting on me to make my move.

"Rise. Take off your dress." My gaze roams her as she discards the material that was covering her body from my view. A shiver trails over her, and I know she's feeling the heat of my stare violating her.

"Drake," she utters my name, causing my body to heat at the word alone. Just hearing her say it in her sweet voice has my slacks tightening. "Please, this isn't you. I know it isn't."

They all plead for their lives. Each one of them wants to go free, wants to be saved by the knight in shining armor.

Sadly, I'm not him.

I'm the beast that will devour them piece by piece.

I stalk around the chair where she's sitting. Her gaze following me, but by the time I'm behind her, I feel the absence of her stare.

Leaning in, I place my lips at her ear and whisper, "There's nothing, and I mean nothing, that will prepare you for what you'll experience in here."

She pulls in a sharp gasp, and I wonder if it's from my words or my warm breath on her sensitive flesh.

"There is no escape. There is no getting out," I tell her. It's the truth. There is no way I can lie to her, because for some unknown fucking reason, this girl has gotten under my skin.

"Do you truly believe that?" she asks without looking over her shoulder at me but twisting her hands in her lap.

"I do, little raven."

She's silent for a moment before she responds,

"You hurt me last night." Her confession burns through me. Every inch of my skin is aflame with rage, but I tamper it down. I'm angry at myself for losing control, but I feel no guilt when the memory of how her mouth felt on my dick assaults me.

I know I'm not allowed to do anything to the girls unless father instructs us, but Caia has a hold on me. A dangerous fucking grip.

"What exactly did I do that you didn't want?" My question is raspy at best, and I hope she doesn't hear the need in my voice. The desire that she innocently elicits from me.

"You shoved your cock into my throat. You were violent."

Hearing her utter those filthy words only serves to make me harder. The image of seeing her choke on my dick makes me throb in my boxers.

"Did it make you wet, little bird?" I question. "Because if it did, I'd certainly enjoy doing that to you again."

"I puked, and no, I did not enjoy it." Her biting remark makes me chuckle. "Are you going to hurt me now?"

"You're not here for me to hurt," I tell her. "The pretty ones are to be savored." I pull out the sleek blade and bring it around so she can see it. "This here is what we're going to play with."

"Please, Drake," she begs again, her voice timid, lower than it was moments ago when she was sassing me.

"I like this part, Caia," I tell her. "When you're scared, your pupils dilate, and those pretty lips part as your breaths come hard and fast."

I smile as she shivers, the cold metal trailing over her bared tits. The sharpness evident in the way it scrapes against her flesh. When I reach her belly button, the tip presses inside. But I'm careful. I know how to use this to either harm or to toy with someone.

"If you move, it will cut you," I warn her. "Be a good girl and stay very still for me." My movements are slow, meticulous, as I reach her panties and slice them from her hips. On either side they fall away. "Open your legs."

She does, and her cunt is bared to me. Beautiful and smooth.

"Oh, darling," I murmur. "How I'd love to eat you right now. Would you like that?" I don't wait for her to respond. "I'd dip my tongue into your tight hole and lick your juices."

She gasps when I nick her with the blade. Watching the sweet crimson drip from the mound of her breast. In a slow trail, it finds her nipple, stopping on the peak, and I lean forward, my tongue lapping at the metallic liquid.

Our gazes lock, the fear in hers sates my beast. It feeds him like never before. It's addicting, not because I enjoy this, but because it's her. She's everything. Her beauty is my tranquility.

The piano plays in the background as I continue trailing my mouth over her flesh. She shivers when I dip my tongue into her belly button. But she watches every moment of my travels. When I finally get to her cunt, I shove her legs open, pressing the knife against the smooth lips, and I wonder just how pretty it would look if my cock was sliding into her in that moment.

I shouldn't be doing this. I shouldn't make her feel good. But her flavor on my tongue is the only thing I can think about. I near her pussy, inhaling her scent, and I know I'm never going to be able to hurt her.

Fuck.

"Tell me your name," I question her. Not moving my face, keeping it near her entrance.

"Caia Amoretto," she confesses in a fearful whisper.

The realization dawns on me when I look up at her from my position between her thighs. She's the one stolen for my father's ultimate job. The music reaches a crescendo, and I breathe her in once more.

I never saw myself as a savior.

I never saw myself as a knight.

But with her beauty, with her name, with everything she is, I'm going to steal her from my father.

I rise, lean in, find her lips, and meld them with

mine. She whimpers when my tongue darts into her warmth, licking and tasting the sweet flavor mixed with the spice of the alcohol she consumed, and I'm addicted.

"Caia," I whisper along her lips. "You've been stolen for a reason."

"Please help me."

Her gaze pierces mine as mine searches hers. I'm eager to have my body against hers, to feel her pulse and tighten, to have her soul entwine with mine, but it's far too dangerous to show I care.

I grip her throat, lifting her from the chair as she flails in my arms. Shock on her features make me smile. As much as I want her, I'm also a sadistic bastard. I shove her against the wall, pressing my body tightly against hers.

"I'm going to fuck you. I'm going to take your virginity and own it. And when I do, you'll be mine."

"Then do it." Her challenge burns through me. "I don't want them to have it. Please?"

"Hearing you beg me to do it makes me even

harder for you. It makes me want to rip into you and make you cry," I utter, and while the words leave my lips, I'm shoving my slacks down, my cock in my fist, and I'm driving into her tight cunt, causing her to cry out from the pain of her hymen tearing as I rip into her.

My hips don't slow. I don't offer her a kiss or kind words. I take it. I fucking own her body, and she lets me. Her nails rake down my neck as she holds on, but she doesn't beg me to stop.

All she does is hold me hostage with her gaze.

And as good as she feels, I know I've truly fucked up now.

Eight
CAIA

ONCE HE'S FOUND RELEASE, HE SETS ME down slowly. He's almost gentle in the way he touches me. Nothing like moments before when he took my virginity.

"That should never have happened," he tells me without meeting my gaze. Those blue orbs are dark as he stares into the distance. Lost in his own world.

"Then it didn't." My words cause him to snap those eyes to mine. "It's done. You've taken it; they can't own it."

"And I can't own you." His counter response does something to my heart. The ache in my chest isn't something I'd like to admit to because I shouldn't feel anything for him. But I do.

"You can leave."

"I can't," he says, pulling at the shirt he was wearing. I watch his fingers button the material, closing off his toned torso to my hungry view.

"Then you'll stay in this hell with the devil beckoning you to do vile things?" My question stills him from pouring two drinks, his hand gripping the crystal decanter, and I'm certain if he doesn't ease up, it will shatter.

"There are things at play here that you know nothing about, little raven." He smirks, filling each shot glass with amber liquid. "Drink this." He hands one to me with a smile that makes my heart stutter.

I take the offered glass and gulp the liquid down in one burning swallow. Tonight shouldn't have happened, but in a way, I'm glad it did. He's taken the one thing they wanted from me, and now, he owns it. And deep down, I know he owns me too.

"I have many secrets, Caia," Drake says sadly as he settles in the wingback chair. "But there are many others who know about them. If I leave, I break promises to people I love."

"Love?"

He chuckles at my raised brow and sips on the alcohol. I set my glass down, then turn to him once more, wanting his blue-eyed gaze on me. It's as if when he takes it away, I am cold, empty.

"I never thought a monster could love," I tell him, goading him to say something, or to do something. I don't know why, but I need it. In this moment, I crave his touch.

"No, you're right." He rises, stalking toward me, causing me to falter and step backward. He's beautiful in his darkness. It shrouds him as if it's attempting to consume him. When he reaches me, my back hits the wall. The same wall he'd just pinned me against. "You see, little bird" — he leans in, our bodies inches from each other — "my life is not filled with sunshine. Hell, it doesn't even have a glimmer of light." Hs words feather over my skin, making me shiver. "But I've accepted it. Just as you've accepted your fate."

"How do you know I have?" Lifting my eyes to his, I find questions dancing in the waves of blue.

"Because you asked me to take what you held onto for so long." It's as if I should've known this would be his answer. "No matter what happens here," he breathes, allowing the heat of his breath to tickle the sensitive skin on my neck. "You'll always be mine."

Nine
DRAKE

SHE'S BEEN HERE FOR TWO WEEKS. SHE'S survived every fucking method of torture, and she's still fighting. I know he's angry, raging that this little girl isn't shattering for him. And soon, she will. He'll pull out all the stops.

My gaze trails over her. There's blood everywhere. She's sleeping, passed out from the pain. I sit at her bedside, my fingertips tracing the scars on her back, on her ass, and down to her feet. The skin the same color as porcelain is bright red with welts. Crimson still drips from the open wounds, and I wonder just how well she did in there.

The fact that she's not dead tells me she's a fighter. I knew she would be. There was a blaze in her beautiful dark eyes that told me she's going to take everything thrown at her and mold it into something that will eventually allow her to fight her way out of here. The only problem is she'll never get out.

We'll all die in this place.

My gaze is locked on her body, the way it lifts and drops as she breathes evenly. Her long hair is matted with something. I'm not sure if it's blood or semen, but it's sticky, making her dark locks knot.

I shiver when she does. Her small feet are curled under her ass, the bones of her spine are protruding against her luminescent flesh. It's a haunting image to see a woman, well, a girl, lie there near death, and even more disturbing to still want her. Still desire her.

The silence hanging in the air is heavy with the chill the concrete walls offer. There are no luxuries in any of the rooms. Each cell — a gray square space that only has one bucket for bodily functions and a steel bed with a worn-out mattress to offer some form of comfort for the girls.

It's been a long while since he brought a boy back. I recall the last boy who came here; he was bought by a man who was in his early fifties.

They're all rich. Each of them with more money than God. And darkness within their souls no amount of prayer can expunge.

"Do you watch?" A voice comes from the bed, startling me. I shift onto my knees, leaning on the edge of the mattress with my gaze glued to the girl.

She shifts, wincing when her body falls onto her back. I want to touch her, to feel her milky skin, but I don't dare. I know if I do, I may not be able to stop. The thought makes me hard. My jeans are uncomfortable now.

Thinking about her pink flesh, open and wet, I cough, hiding the groan that rumbles in my chest.

"You're hurt," I tell her, stating the obvious. I admonish myself silently. I feel almost immature beside her. I don't know how to be around a woman. Especially one who makes me feel things without being in the *dungeon* where my father forced the most horrific things on me. The psychological games he plays are for his *clients* to benefit from. The depraved acts the men and women who come in here to experience are far worse than anyone can imagine.

With each session he administers on the girls, he ensures they're no longer able to fight back. That they're just broken toys. And he made sure I'm as cold as he is, but what he doesn't know is I still have my heart. He may have darkened my soul, but I'm a lot stronger than he gives me credit for. *And he just doesn't need to find out what I did to Caia.*

The mansion he's owned all his life, inherited from my grandad, is beautiful, decked in expensive furniture, but what people don't know is the darkness lurking beneath. The rooms where the girls are held, and the dungeon where the sessions happen, have been hidden from plain sight. When the clients arrive, they enter through a secret door and exit from it as well.

I look at the girl once more. She offers me a small

smile. It's an honest, sweet gesture which angers me. There's something about her that makes me weak, makes me want to kiss and hold her.

I rise to my full height, stalking toward the corner, then back again. I do so a few times, pacing. There's an ache in my chest, and I hit it with my fist. As hard as I can, I continue the attack, but it does nothing to help my desires.

"What are you doing?" she questions from behind me. I can't look at her. I'm so fucked up, the moment I turn I'll hurt her. I'll fucking break her just to hear her cry. And it's not because I like hurting her, but it's the only way I know how. My mind has been fragmented so many times the only way I know how to get off is by pain, inflicting it, watching someone do it. I hear the springs of the bed creak, and I'm certain she's going to come to me.

"Don't come near me." My command is harsh, as cold as the room we're in. I'm dressed in warm clothes, jeans, socks, and boots, with a heavy woolen hoodie. But the girl, the pretty dolly, is only dressed in panties.

They're also bloody. I'd looked at them earlier. I'd traced my finger over them while I'd jerked my dick. I'd stroked myself in my fist while I touched her bloody cunt.

"Why are you being like this? After what we did?" she questions, but she doesn't come near me. Her obedience is perfect, just what he'd like. The man who's now her owner until someone comes along and pays good money for her.

"Don't act like we're a couple, little bird. You're a good fuck. Don't go falling in love with me."

"I don't fall in love with monsters," she says softly. "I have no choice but to be here, it seems. All I wanted was to talk to someone. After what happened between us, I thought—"

"You thought wrong, so stop talking and just let me finish up in here. Tomorrow, you're going to be taken back to him. There's no longer anything I can do."

I still, turning to face her. The movement is slow, almost wary because I don't know if she's actually there. If she's real. But I did fuck her. I felt her break around my cock, and I savored it. I reveled in taking her violently, and she in turn moaned my name even though she didn't come.

"My father is the owner of a tech company in Miami," she starts talking again, but I ignore her. "But, I mean, he's not a good person." She sighs, the sound sad, but there's also frustration clear in her tone. "Is this because of him? What am I doing here? Please, talk to me." She looks at me as she questions me as if I should feel something for her.

I don't.

My nonresponse is met with a gentle gaze. We're not friends. We never will be. She won't live long enough to be anything to me, but the way she regards me, it's as if I've known her my whole life.

A knock on the door has her shooting to the bed, the squeaky springs under the threadbare mattress echo in the room, and I cringe. I don't know who's at the door, but all I can hope for is that it's not my father.

When I pull it open, I find my best friend standing

on the other side.

"Hey," he says, his lopsided grin greeting me, and I exhale, allowing the tension in my shoulders to ease slightly.

"Does he know you're here?" River shakes his head and glances over my shoulder. I know he can see her, and I wonder if he's jealous that I'm here and not in bed. "Did you want to head out?"

I shake my head no. I should want to go, but the thought of leaving Caia alone here only sets my nerves on edge.

"Hi." Her voice is sweet behind me as she greets River.

He pushes by me, entering the small space, and I grip the handle of the door in fear, hoping my father doesn't decide to walk down to the girls' cells to check up on them this morning. I glance at the time on my wristwatch and note it's almost five in the morning. He'll be here soon.

"We can't stay long."

River nods in understanding. We both watch Caia for a moment as if she's the show and we're paid attendees.

"Will I see you tomorrow?" Her question jars me. None of the other girls who have been in here have ever asked me that.

"Maybe." I tug open the door, leaving enough space for River to exit, and I follow him out. I don't look at her again when I click the door shut behind me.

"You like her," he observes.

I shrug, not looking at him as I respond, "She'll be dead tomorrow."

Ten
CAIA

ALONE.

I've been alone for a long while. I can't tell if it's night or day. The space I'm in offers some artificial light, but I can't see outside. The thick concrete walls have kept me prisoner. My back aches. It stings as I move, and I try my best to recall what happened when I was bound to the metal bed.

"You're such a pretty little toy," a gruff voice from behind me speaks. A small trolley is rolled closer. On it is a computer, which is currently black. The screen is dead, and I wish I was.

I'm still sick from the images I saw earlier. From the girl being beheaded. There was a sick satisfaction on the man's face as he did it, as if he found pleasure in doing what he did.

I don't speak now. I know it's pointless. A cold device is pressed against me, and I feel my body opening, the object slipping inside my core.

"She's a virgin," the man says. I can't tell the difference between the two anymore. There's no distinct change in tone, and I wonder if I'm losing my mind. A small sharp prick against my shoulder shoots something warm and languid through me. My muscles are limp, and I find I can no longer move my limbs.

"There, there," a voice coos. Then a large, hairy hand reaches for the computer, and the screen lights up with images. Scrolling from one to the next of similar scenes to earlier, it plays on a loop, and I can't move my eyes. They're watering from tears, but I can't close them.

That's when a vibrating object is placed at my entrance. Against the spot of my body that sends pleasurable tingles through me.

"You'll learn to play the game, little one," the man tells me with confidence. A click sounds behind me, but I can't move.

Frozen. Captive. A prisoner. I'm stolen.

When the screen changes, a video appears full screen, and the tears I'd been blinking away burn a path down my cheeks onto the cold metal gurney.

Once more, a man walks on screen. As he undresses, something is pushed inside me, tearing through me so harshly I cry out, the sound ricocheting off the walls.

The sound is turned up on the computer, and I'm met with the old man grunting inside the throat of a girl who looks so familiar. A girl whom I've known my whole life. And I recall the moment the man moves to offer us a view of her pretty green eyes—the image of my sister.

There's blood dripping from her nose, but she's lying upside down, and I watch in horror as she's violated once more by the man who turns to the camera and chuckles as his cock is lodged in her throat.

My heart catapults wildly when his face comes on screen, and the vibrator against my clit is turned up harshly, causing pleasure and pain to skitter through me like a ten-pound weight.

An orgasm rocks me when I look into the eyes of my father, and all I can do is succumb to the force of agony that I'm thoroughly fucking broken. I've been torn from a normal life. I'm severed.

The door creaks open, and I'm met with the deep blue eyes of the man who has been my captor for the past few days . . . weeks? His dark hair is a stark contrast to the asphalt color walls. He doesn't say anything, merely shuts the door and heads to the bucket in the corner. It's empty. I haven't eaten anything in the past few days. I don't recall drinking anything either. My body is weak, and I know there's no way I can fight my way out of here.

"You'll get lunch shortly," he bites out coldly. There's something strange about him, something I can't place my finger on. When he turns to regard me once more, he sees my face is glistening in the low light of the oil lamp he's carrying. "Are you crying?"

I don't want to tell him I am. I don't want to admit to feeling broken, shattered. I don't want to tell him what

I saw. But something tells me he knows. Surely, he does.

"I asked you a question."

"Yes, of course I'm crying. I'm locked in hell with the devil and his foot soldiers, and I am wounded beyond repair."

He stalks toward me, and I'm certain he's going to hurt me, but he stops just short of my bed. He leans in close, his face right in mine. I meet those eyes that remind me of freedom, of the clear blue sky and the cool ocean waters.

"If you cry, he'll only make it worse."

"What do you care?" I bite out in frustration.

"Did you come when you watched the video?" he smirks. A cold, cruel grin curls his lips. "Did your little cunt get all wet and achy?" He leans in closer, his mouth almost on mine. "And when you came, did you cry out for God?"

"Fuck you!" I spit, the clear saliva hitting his face just below one of his beautiful eyes. The man is sinful, like the devil in disguise.

"Your next training session is today. After lunch, you'll learn just how much worse it can get." With that, he spins on his heel, and I want to crawl to him and beg him to free me. My mind is awash with confusion, everything is blurry and cloudy. The door opens. Another young man walks inside carrying a tray. He sets it on the bed beside me and they leave me alone.

I don't know what to do, but the food on the tray is my only sustenance, and I wolf it down in the hopes it will strengthen me. I need to fight. I have to get out of here.

The bread is soft and warm, the butter melting on it making my mouth water. I stuff it in my mouth, not bothering to chew. I need to eat, and the ravenous feeling overwhelms me. Tears trickle from my eyes once more as I revel in the flavors on my tongue.

I drink the water from the mug on the tray. It satiates my thirst like I've been given life once more. Moments later the tray is empty. I lift it in order to place it on the floor, but as soon as I attempt to stand, my legs give out and I fall to my knees, the metal clanking loudly. My ears feel as if they're about to shatter, and that's when my eyes flutter closed once more.

Eleven
DRAKE

"**Y**OU'RE READY, SON." MY FATHER GLARES at me. Malcolm has been a man of many faces. Most think he's an upstanding citizen, but those who know who he truly is, down to his rotten soul, they're the ones who respect him more than anything. They fear him. They fucking love him.

And you know why?

Because he offers them what they want. Fantasies that would make the most fucked-up asshole cringe.

Depraved.

Vile.

Filthy.

"You want me to do it?"

He snaps his gaze to me, those blue orbs that

match mine and Dante's pierce me, and I feel it down to my fucking soul. At twenty-five, I should be out chasing girls and partying up a storm. Instead, he's imprisoned me as much as he has the rest of those who work here.

"If you're a pussy and can't do it, you can watch," he grunts, waving his hand at Ivor who's been in this dungeon for more than eight years. The large man who resembles an ogre is fast on his feet, and he's got me in a grip so tight it steals my breath.

"I can, just let me go, Dad," I try to reason with him, but he's already got the opera playing through the speakers. "Ivor, just let me go. I can do the training." All my pleading falls on deaf ears. As much as I've been working for my father, he's still in charge. I'm pushed onto a steel contraption similar to the seating at a sports stadium at the far wall, which offers me a clear view of the table he's about to mutilate Caia on.

A flannel gag is shoved into my mouth, and I spit it out immediately. Ivor knows better than to attempt this shit with me. He may be my father's right-hand man, but

I'm the son of Malcolm Savage, and one day I'll make sure he pays for the shit he's done.

The door flies open, and one of my father's men stalks in with her passed out, and I realize the lunch she'd eaten must've ensured it. She's placed on the table; a cold, metal surgeon's table, and my body turns rigid.

Another person is brought inside, and I meet his gaze. My best friend. The only person who's stood by me besides my brother. I hope Dante doesn't come downstairs. He doesn't need to watch this. Even though we're the same age bar a couple of minutes in between, I feel overly protective of my brother.

"You shouldn't be here," I hiss at River who finds his place beside me.

"I'm not letting you go through this alone." His words are a salve. But I know they'll never heal the brokenness inside me.

"Ah, young River. You're here to enjoy the show?" My father glares at him, and I know he doesn't like my best friend. We've never learned who River's family is, and over the years, he's become like part of the family. Only, I know my feelings for my best friend run far deeper.

I know it's about to go downhill when two men stalk into the space, bodyguards, and they're followed by three men and two women. All dressed immaculately, they seat themselves not far from the table.

We're not to move. My father's rules have always been very specific. Even though I can physically walk out of here at any moment, I know I can't because he'll do something he's threatened me with all my life. He'll kill River and Dante. Two people who mean more to me than anything. So, I sit.

Watching the scene play out before me. One I've watched so many times. The girl is lifted onto an apparatus that has her bound to an X-shaped wooden cross. She's naked, and her supple body causes my cock to throb.

That's why we're all broken here. Our minds have been fractured, and in the gaps where sanity should lie, we've been drenched in the depravity. Her eyes flutter open, and they land on mine as if they're opposite poles of a magnet.

Twelve

CAIA

THE GATHERING WATCHES ME CRY. THE HEAT of the blood dripping from between my legs scorches me. I can't move, my legs are useless, my brain screaming at them to do something, but they can't.

"Please," I whimper. It's almost inaudible, but he hears me. I know he does. All I receive in response is a chuckle. I'm shut down, completely numb, I feel nothing. I pray for my end. I pray for the pain. Perhaps it will wake me from this nightmare. Maybe, just maybe, I can be saved, and this is all just in my mind. But how would my imagination think up the depraved acts that have been happening?

"What do you think, ladies?" he questions the onlookers. The two women dressed in beautiful evening gowns have the material bunched up to their hips with their legs spread wide and two boys who look to be my age between their thighs. The men seated beside the women have their gazes locked on me. Their hands move over their thick erections as they grunt and smirk, looking at me with the hunger of wolves. They're predators, nothing but animals.

"Why don't we test her ability for pain? If I'm going to spend ten million on a toy, I'd want to make sure she can handle a bit of rough." One man offers me a wink that recoils my stomach. The incisions on my stomach already burn with the puke dripping from my chin, but when one of the women finds her release, she grips the boy's head, and just like in the movie they forced me to watch, she pulls a sleek blade from the holster on her thigh and slices through his neck as if it's a hot knife cutting through butter.

Revulsion shoots through me when I'm impaled with the thick handle of a blade used only moments ago to trail blood-red lines over my white flesh. My eyes flutter. I'm weary. This is far too much for me to handle. I can no longer hold on. He told me I was stupid to fight back, to resist, and now I believe him.

I glance at the man who looked at me with more affection than I've ever experienced. His lips move, his mouth tells me something, but I can't hear. I can't read his lips.

He shakes his head sadly as he watches the scene unfold. He told me I was going to be in trouble. If I cried, only worse would happen, and he's right. Well, he was right because I'm losing consciousness.

The men were here to get off from the pain they inflicted.

Another girl is brought in. She is younger, smaller, but the two large men don't care. Once more, I'm hooked up to a vibrator that offers pleasure, pressed tightly against my mound as I watch the gruesome scene before me.

The girl is pretty; she giggles as if she's high. Perhaps she is and doesn't even realize she's about to be killed. I open my mouth, but I'm quickly stopped by the large ogre-looking man. There's a harsh material shoved into my mouth, and I'm choking on the fine filaments of hair and the taste of metallic residue. I'm certain it's blood, but what makes me retch is the fact that I know it's not mine.

"Shhh, little one. Tonight you'll see what it is we really do here," the ogre tells me proudly. The girl is bound to the table before me, her legs are spread wide, and I watch as one of the women walks up to her. It's the same one who just killed a boy.

She leans in, inspecting the girl as if she were a painting at the Louvre. Her fingers trail down the smooth porcelain flesh of the young girl. When she reaches between her legs, she nods, prodding the girl's opening.

A giggle falls from the girl's lips, and I know for a fact they've given her something. There's no way she can be happy with her body on display like that. Her eyes are wide, glassy. She's drugged so much that she can't focus on me. Her eyes flit left and right, her body also limp on the silver gurney. Another giggle falls from her lips, but she doesn't speak, as if she can't. When the woman grips her chin and tugs it open, I recoil at the sight of her missing tongue. The burning acid that trails up my throat makes my eyes water in my attempt to swallow it down.

"Is she to your specifications?" The old man grins like the fucking Cheshire cat.

"She is. I'll need this done tonight," the woman responds. I don't know what is happening, but the girl is bound to the table, and as the older man places a silver scalpel to her stomach, he presses down, and crimson floods the table immediately.

"How far along is she?" the second woman questions as she rises, pulling the boy that was between her thighs along behind her like a dog on a leash.

"Two months. It's just the perfect amount of time," the man in the white coat informs her.

"Good. Then we'll take whatever you can salvage." I'm tortured with the device between my legs as the man in the white coat begins his incisions to the girl's body below her belly button. I stare in horror as he slices through her flesh easily.

She's numb, because there are no screams, no cries or whimpers from her. She doesn't feel anything. Her body is limp as he lifts a layer of her stomach and shoves his hand into her.

That's when she starts gurgling. It's a vicious sound, her body convulsing, and one of the men who was merely observing rises, shoves down his zipper, and pushes his cock into her mouth. Her throat bulges obscenely as the scene is set before them, as if they're watching a porn video.

My own body responds to the vibrator on my clit, but my stomach heaves. My head is once again cloudy, foggy as confusion sets in. My scream is muffled by the cloth, my body tightens and pulses as an orgasm wracks through me as I witness the man in the white coat pull the womb from the young girl, and I realize they were talking about her being pregnant.

How far along is she?

Two months.

The perfect amount of time.

Thirteen
DRAKE

Today is the end. I can feel it in my bones.

"I thought you said she'd be dead," River whispers from beside me. I'm so numb I don't even notice the scene before me. I sit like the mechanical robot he's turned me into. My heart thuds as I watch her. I want to cry, to go to her, but I can never fight all of them off, even with River and Dante's help.

"I did say that. I lied."

I feel his gaze on me. It's burning through my flesh, turning my body tense and rigid. He's the only person I've ever allowed to come near me. To touch me. After what I'd been through, I no longer enjoy the gentle caress of another, and I don't offer it either.

"I need to do something."

That doesn't mean I haven't fucked my dick into some of the corpses. Those who are cold and rigid. I can't handle warmth anymore. It's not who I am. I'm a monster, and as the girl's womb is ripped from her body, I feel nothing.

I sit.

I watch.

I feel a pulse in my dick. I'm hard. Turned on by the depravity. Because he made me that way. He's forced me, just like he's forcing her, Caia, to feel desire at the sick deeds. Only she doesn't know why.

I do.

I know all his moves. And soon, I'll make sure that he takes his last breath. I won't do it quickly.

No.

I'll revel in the slow torture of his filthy flesh. Those pieces of him he finds pleasure in, I'll ensure they're burned while still attached.

How beautiful it will be.

The bright orange flame dancing along the

wrinkled old skin of his cock. I'm lost in my violent thoughts, so I don't notice when he has Ivor drag Caia over to the table that the dead girl has just vacated.

"Do it." River's voice cuts through the clouds in my head. I'm not even sure how he managed to fuck with my head so much, but he has. He's broken me. "Drake, if you don't do something now, you'll lose the girl."

It's only when her muffled screams seem to jolt me into action that I realize I'm moving. My feet are racing to her, watching as he brings his scalpel down onto her smooth stained and bruised flesh. There's a man fucking her throat, violating the tight hole that I want.

I realize then that I want her.

I need her.

"No!"

My father's gaze snaps to mine with a fury I've never seen before.

He smirks, pressing the cool metal against her pretty face. Her beautiful cheek is soon oozing crimson liquid, the color of Merlot I have at the dinner table.

"I knew you were a fucking pussy," my father grunts. There's a cock of a weapon, the click of a barrel, and I lose all sense of what I'm doing. It feels as if my body is slowing down when I reach her.

I grasp her hand, pulling her from the metal table and onto the floor. Her throat is turning blue, the convulsions wracking through her are violent, and the pungent stench of puke falls onto my chest as she expels the drugs they've clearly injected into her.

It's then that I see it.

Behind her.

The man who was using her throat like a cunt pulls the weapon, and its only seconds before I register the shot. It sears through her, into me, and I cry out in agony when I realize I've just lost the first thing I ever wanted to care for.

The only thing I wanted to nurture.

And her limp body is now on top of me.

Are you ready to be
SEVERED?

CONTINUE THE STORY IN SEVERED

Blurb

*This is NOT a standalone. You need to read Stolen - The
Prequel to fully understand this storyline.*

My world was hell on earth, son of a man who was evil incarnate.
Hate was all I knew.

When she was stolen, I swore I'd find her.
When I meet her eyes again, I remember what I'm fighting for.
The girl will be mine.

***

I've seen true evil, held captive by the devil himself.
And now revenge is all I know.

Everything was stolen from me. Until him.
When my eyes meet his, I'm caught in his web.
Each moment that passes only confirms what I already know
—I'm his.

*This is a dark romance. Due to scenes of an adult nature, this
book is for 18 ONLY. That's the only warning you'll get.*

Prologue
DRAKE

The sins of the father fall to the son.

Violence has been in my blood since I was born.

Love has never been something I wanted, needed, or thought of. I smile when I think about the one girl who almost managed to weasel her way into my heart, but she was stolen from me. Our link was severed, and I became the monster my father wanted me to be.

I buried my feelings for her along with the memory of her body bleeding out on top of me. The images haunted me each night. They replayed in my mind, but after my search for her came to a dead end. I locked away that damned muscle called my heart. Securing it in a cage,

I ensured I'd never allow anyone to ever free it again.

I'm a Savage.

I'm the heir to a throne that was never my choice. It was forced upon me, and even though I shouldn't want it, I have no choice. The moment my father took his last breath, I knew I was never going to be free.

Dante, my brother, wants me to stop the Savage Organization. He's begged and pleaded, but what he doesn't understand is there's always more to a story than meets the eye.

I'm doing this for him. For me. For our family. If only he can give me time, I'll show him that the secrets that lie locked within the walls of the mansion hold so much more.

River, my best friend and part-time lover, is the only one who knows why I stay, why I continue in the legacy left by my father, Malcolm Savage. And he's the only one who can help me.

Sometimes, we must do things we don't want to.

We do things that will ensure our morals are

challenged.

And, at other times, we do things to keep those we love safe.

One
DRAKE

GAMES.
Sick, twisted games.

I spent my childhood learning how to play them.

He taught me. Turned me into a monster. He played them with me. I witnessed horrors that will forever be stained in my mind. Those vile images I've tried so hard to tamper, they rage within me, like a fire taking out a forest. Each night, I close my eyes, and those eyes haunt me. As much as I've tried, I can never stop them.

Guilt sits within my gut. It burns its way through my blood. I can never be free from the nightmares, and perhaps I don't want to be. It's those memories that allow me to do what I do. To finally attempt to rid my hands of the blood my father spilled.

The dark web my father had built for his organization still runs today. With new clients messaging me each day, I know time is running out before they realize I'm leading them on. I don't have much longer to keep them at bay. The monsters are beating down the door, and soon, I'm going to have to let them in.

Bit by bit, as the days passed and the older I got, the more I lost myself. I knew if I didn't get away soon, there'd be nothing left of the boy I was. For years, he got away with what he did. My only escape was my bedroom, where I would lose myself in River, in his touch, his body. And if he wasn't around, I'd silently sit in the shadows and watch Dante like a fucking stalker. He would have one of his latest conquests around, and I'd dive into the darkness with them. A voyeur to pleasure. It was the only way I could feel again.

I'm broken. I'm a fucked-up monster. And there's no longer anything that can change me. Four years ago, I thought there was a chance. I believed I could be someone different because of her. A girl with the most beautiful soul I'd ever seen. She weakened me, and I almost let myself go. I wanted to steal her away, keep her for myself. But in the end, it was she who was stolen from me.

Her blood still stains my hands. The metallic taste of her life essence still coats my tongue. She bled out, her slight frame draped over me. One moment she was there. The next, she was gone.

The video I've been watching is on a loop. The body of the girl onscreen is bruised as one of the guards gets her ready for tonight's show. I'm lost in the darkness as my hand finds my hardened cock. I blame my father for this. He broke my mind, leaving only shattered fragments of my innocence.

I am no longer my own person. He owned me in ways I forced to the back of my mind. With each vile act I endured, he made sure that my only escape was to die. But I couldn't give up my life. I had to be there for Dante and River.

Instead of running, I planned. Each day and night that passed, I made sure I had everything I needed to take him down. His friends, partners, all of them would suffer. I would make sure of it.

Everything he did to me, all those things he made me witness, I'll perhaps never forget, but I can clear my conscience by killing the assholes who supported him. My father died from the wounds I inflicted only six months ago. We've kept the news from everyone because my plan can finally start.

Revenge.

Such a beautiful word.

Blood will be spilled. I will bathe in it. Drench myself in the metallic liquid because that's what they deserve. I played hide and seek from a young age. I hid as best I could from the men and women who frequented our estate. And now that my father has met his maker, I'll ensure those filthy pieces of trash answer to me.

And only me.

I'll run a rampage through his organization so

violent, so bloody that no one can save them. And when I walk away with their blood staining my hands, I'll have my vengeance.

It took years to learn, to observe their movements. Each small nuance is ingrained in my mind. It makes me more dangerous than they can ever be. It makes me the killer they never saw coming.

"Are you listening to me?"

The voice drags me from the horrors replaying in my mind on a loop. I glance at the light eyes that match mine and nod. My brother, Dante Savage, is all grown up now. I haven't been listening to a word he said. But I nod in any case.

"Drake, we can do this together," he tells me, placing a hand on my shoulder. Dante wants something I can never have. He's told me before how he wants to find a girl and settle down. Strangely, I can see him doing that, but the problem is, those dark desires that seem to ignite when he's fucking someone have always scared them away. I want to laugh when I think about my volatile brother, but then I realize, in all my years trying to protect him, I didn't do a very good job because he's just as fucked up as I am.

"You need to stay here, make sure they don't come looking for Malcolm," I inform him once more as I watch the screen. I know Dante can see my hard-on. There's nothing hidden between us. We've both witnessed each other in our worst states. We've shared women. We've shared River. Our sexuality is nothing like anyone else's. Our minds don't work right. And after the childhood we've had, nobody can blame us.

"Do you still look for her?"

I know he's talking about Caia. The girl I wanted. The one who attempted to make me feel. Perhaps I did. But then she was stolen, severed from my life before I had a chance to really know her. Even though we've searched for her high and low, I now believe she's never coming back.

Our lives are filled with darkness. Hers was only light. If only I wasn't late in stopping my father that night,

I would never have lost her. I could've fucking saved her. And every time I think about it, I hate myself more. She didn't deserve what happened.

"No. She's dead." My cold words cause him to flinch; only slightly, but I see it. As much as Dante plays the hard-ass, I know deep down he's not like me. Nowhere near.

"And what if one day you walk into a house and find her there? Are you going to finish the job father failed to do?" he questions me. "Or will you admit you fell for her?"

"I fucking told you time and again," I bite out, turning to pin him with an angry glare. "She's dead."

"If you say so," he utters. "I don't believe she is, because father would've had a file on her burial spot, like he does with everyone else he's killed." Could she be alive? I almost believe him. Only for a moment I allow my mind to wonder how it would feel to find her, to feel her touch, her lips. I let myself feel happiness, normality. But in the same second it appears, it's gone.

Since the moment I walked into the cell and laid my eyes on Caia, I felt my world tilt off its axis. Not one other girl who had been brought here made me want to protect and hurt her in equal measure. She fed the hunger my father ingrained in me. He's turned me into this. A sick monster who yearns to see the vile acts being portrayed before me.

Dante keeps me sated in his own way. He allows me to watch, to be a voyeur, and through him and River, I find release when I need it.

I still want to hurt though. There's nothing like seeing shimmering tears on pretty porcelain flesh. To see pouty lips wrapped tightly around my cock until tears drench rosy cheeks. I still get hard when I think of depraved acts. There is no help for me anymore. Nothing can remove what's embedded in my mind.

If anyone witnessed what I have, they could never be sane.

"Let's get this meeting underway. I have somewhere to be tonight," I tell my brother. I need to feed this desire, and there's only one way to do it. To visit the cells. I need it like a shot of heroin to the vein.

And as we walk out the door, I feel almost normal once more.

Almost.

But I know I'll never be again.

Two
DRAKE

I'M STILL FRUSTRATED FROM OUR MEETING ONLY an hour ago with one of the biggest clients my father had. The man that's next on my list. I've planned how I want him to die, and watching him play "happy family" with his wife tonight makes me want to rip his perfect life apart. Knowing tomorrow night, when River and I head out there again with my team I'll get to watch his blood drip from the wounds I inflict, it makes me hard.

The room I enter is bathed in darkness. I can barely see the small form of the pretty toy huddled in the corner. As soon as Malcolm died, I changed how things run in this house.

"Get up," I bite out, my voice booming through

the dark space. The girl's small body shoots up from the mattress. She's dressed in a thin, white cotton nightdress, and I know she's not wearing anything underneath.

"Please, don't hurt me, he . . . he's already . . ." I know what she wants to tell me, but I'm not here to fuck her. I'm here to watch. I can't do shit to any of them, and it pisses me off. As much as I want to be the monster, I can't even do that right.

"I said get the fuck up." My words are a low growl vibrating through my chest as I stalk toward her. Those dark eyes widen, and for a moment I'm taken back in time. To her. To Caia.

She attempts to crawl away, but I'm far too quick for her, and my fingers wrap around her thin arm. Tugging her to the edge of the bed, I lean in and flick the switch against the wall.

The yellow light illuminates her face, and I stare at her for far too long. Her eyes fill with tears when she sees me. Her lips are full, pouty, and as much as I want to feed her my dick, I know it's not going to bring me the satisfaction I want.

"Open your legs." My order is clear when I release her and step back. I pull the chair closer to the bed and settle on the seat. She's still frozen in place, and I know she's in shock that I'm not hurting her.

"I . . . I—"

"I said open your fucking legs," I grit out through clenched teeth. When she finally obeys, I smile, noticing her smooth-shaven little cunt. She trembles before me, and it only makes me harder. "Spread them wider," I order, and she silently submits to me. I wonder then if she's only doing it because I'm not hurting her or trying to shove my cock in her tiny hole. "You're a good girl." I smile. "Now finger yourself."

Her pouty lips part on a soft gasp that makes me throb behind my zipper. Tentatively, she moves her hand between her legs, but she doesn't do anything further. I wonder if she's ever done it. Surely, she's not that innocent.

"You've never touched yourself?"

She shakes her head, her cheeks darkening as she watches me. Her sweet innocence is similar to that of Caia's. She may be scared, but she's not a doormat. I love fire in a girl, her fight, and that stubbornness that only makes me harder every time I taunt her.

"Do it," I insist, nudging my chin toward her. "Put your index finger inside. Feel your warmth." My eyes are glued to the juncture between her thighs. Her toes curl into the mattress when her digit disappears inside her tight core.

A soft whimper falls from her lips, and my cock jolts with the need to take her, but I don't. I never can. She continues to finger herself while I palm my dick, watching the way her eyelashes flutter on the apples of her cheeks.

"Stop." My command has her gaze snapping to mine, her hand frozen between her legs. "I'm not a nice man."

She nods. "I know."

"How do you know that, pet?"

She's silent for a long while, her eyes never straying from mine. Her lips part, and I expect an answer, but all she does is inhale a deep breath, then let it out before shutting her mouth.

"Take your fingers and lick your juices off," I tell her.

Quietly, she complies, and the sight has me groaning. She moves to close her legs, but I shake my head.

"Do you want to go home?" My question has her pretty brown eyes lighting up. She nods, a small smile playing on her full lips. "Do you want to go see your mommy and daddy?"

"Fuck you," she bites back when I taunt her. "I hate you."

Rising, I button my suit jacket, take a step, and lean over her. Fisting her strands, I tug her closer, pulling her against me. She attempts to get free, but I'm far too strong.

"I like when you fight. It makes my dick hard," I

smirk. She stills, her gaze burning into me, and all I see is Caia. Leaning in, I run my lips along her wet cheek, my tongue darting out to lick her tears. The salty liquid igniting a primal need deep within me, and I know if I don't walk out of this room now, I'll fuck her. I'll hurt her. I've always taken women who remind me of the one woman who made me love. As much as I want to offer love, I can't.

Cold settles in my veins, reminding me that I'm not him. I'm not the monster I grew up with. I can be better. I can be more than the asshole who fucked up so many lives.

Shoving her away from me onto the mattress, I turn and stalk toward the door. In the hallway, I lean against the wall and breathe through the desire to maim. Sighing, I make my way up to my bedroom. My mind is still on the girl when I find River asleep on the bed. His form is relaxed, and the comfort of his soft breaths calms me somewhat. There are times I wonder how you can stay so loyal to a person when they can never offer you what you need.

Tomorrow, I'll start my reign of destruction, and soon enough, I'll free Dante and River from this life. And hopefully, I'll save myself in the process.

I settle beside him in the silence. I want to reach for him, to feel him in my arms, but I don't. I shove my feelings deep down so nobody can find them. Not even me.

When I first realized how I felt about River, I was scared. There wasn't anything I could do anyway. No relationship would've been enough to apologize for the life he'd been forced into. So, I pushed him away.

There was only one thing I could give him. One way of saying sorry for all the years of pain. Staring up at the ceiling, I recall the moment we freed ourselves from Malcolm's grip.

The room where my father has been lying in bed for the past few months stinks of death. Over the past six months, I've been slipping poison in his food. I've spent my life learning how to kill him. I wanted to make sure he suffered with every breath he took, and now as I stare at the withering body of the man who was once formidable, I realize my work is done.

"You were always stronger than your brother," he croaks when I near him. His hands are wrinkled, the skin pallid. His hair has grayed and has mostly fallen out. The balding old man is no longer scary. He's scared.

"I was stronger than you."

"You are certainly more intelligent than I gave you credit for, Drake." He attempts to laugh, but the wheeze on his chest makes it sound like he's about to die any second. "This life was something I didn't want."

"You could've fooled me."

"Drake, there is always more to what you see on the surface," he informs me, lifting a shaky hand toward me.

I don't move, and he lowers his reach. "I don't need a lecture from you today, Malcolm," I tell him. "It's time you left us forever."

"You can never take back what you do today, son."

"I don't ever want to take this back. I never want to

forget when I see the light flicker from your eyes. I'll remember it for the rest of my life." Finally closing the distance between me and the bed, I look at Malcolm Savage. Seeing him alive for the last time is something I've waited for since the moment I learned who my father was.

The door behind me creaks open, and their footsteps near me. The two men who will stand beside me as we do this. Dante leans in, his face close to our father's. I'm not sure what he's about to do, then he lifts his hand, twisting the kitchen knife my father enjoyed using when he tortured someone.

"Goodbye, Daddy Dearest." His grin is manic when he pushes the tip of the knife into Malcolm's left eye, causing blood to spurt from the wound. He twists it around as the old man cries out in agony.

Next, River reaches for his other eye, holding it open so he can't blink. "This is for me, for the two men I love, and for all those who came before and after us." He tilts the small, amber glass bottle and drips out three clear drops of acid, which only makes my father's groans of agony echo around us.

His mutilated face makes me smile. If only Caia were

still here, still alive to witness the scene before me. I would've bent her over this bed and fucked her into oblivion while my father died.

Dante and River step back as I take the rope and tie it around his neck, ensuring the knot is tight, I tug on the leash-like twine and drag his body off the bed. Only when I reach the door do I feel it. The sag. No more fight, no more life.

Malcolm Savage is dead.

Ackowledgments
THANK YOU

This was the darkest story I've ever written, so far. It appeared in the When the Dark Wins anthology, and when readers begged for more, I thought I'd have to tell Drake and Caia's story.

Thank you for diving into the dark with me and I hope you enjoy Severed and learn more about what happens after.

Thank you to my BETA's—Alicia, Allyson, Cat— you ladies are amazing. I don't know how I could do this without you!

A huge thanks to my my Angels street team—Tre, Sheena, Sarah, Lisa, Caroline, TJ, Hayfaah, Joy, Cinders, Kathy, Sara, Tanya—thank you for pimping my work EVERYWHERE. You ladies rock!!

To my adult, Diane, thank you for everything! Thanks for keeping me in line and ensuring I don't completely lose it!

My reader group, The Darklings, as always, you're the only place I know I'll find like-minded ladies and a handful of gents who will have a laugh without drama. The group has grown so much and I'm excited for the future! Thank you for being there.

To all my author colleagues, thank you for always sharing, commenting, and supporting me. I appreciate every one of you. Having a support system is important and you ladies provide that and so much more.

Readers and bloggers, from the bottom of my little black heart, THANK YOU. All you do for us authors is incredible. Reading and reviewing is demanding on your own time and you do it with a smile. Thank you so, so much. You are valued and appreciated for taking time out to show us so much love.

If you enjoyed this story, please consider leaving a review. I'd love you forever. (Even though I already do!)

About
THE AUTHOR

Dani is a *USA Today* bestselling author of a variety of genres,
from romantic suspense to dark erotic romance and even
BDSM romance. She loves to delve into the raw, emotional
journeys her characters venture on, and enjoys the dark, edgy,
and sensual scenes that fill the pages of her books. Dani's
stories are seductive with a deviant edge with feisty heroines
and dominant alphas.

Dani lives in the beautiful city of Cape Town, and is a proud
member of the Romance Writer's Organization of South
Africa (ROSA) and the Romance Writers of America (RWA).
She has a healthy addiction to reading, TV series, music,
tattoos, chocolate, and ice cream.

Find me
ONLINE

Do you follow me?
If not, head over to any of the below links,
I love to hear from my readers!

Newsletter: https://goo.gl/xx3bbj

Website: www.danirene.com

Facebook: http://bit.ly/DaniFBPage

Twitter: http://bit.ly/DaniTwitter

Instagram: http://bit.ly/DaniIG

BookBub: http://bit.ly/DaniBookBub

Goodreads: http://bit.ly/DaniGoodreads

Amazon: http://bit.ly/DaniAmazon

Pinterest: http://bit.ly/DaniPinterest

Tumblr: http://bit.ly/DaniTumblr

Book - Main Bites: http://bit.ly/Book_Main

Spotify: http://bit.ly/DaniSpotify

Other books
BY ME

Malignus (Inferno World Novella)
Virulent (collaboration with Yolanda Olson)
Tempting Grayson

Sins of Seven Series
Kneel (Book #1)
Obey (Book #2)
Indulge (Book #3)
Ruthless (Book #4)
Bound (Book #5)
Envy (Book #6)
Vice (Book #7)

The Stolen Series
Stolen
Severed

Four Fathers Series
Kingston

Four Sons Series
Brock

Carina Press Novellas
Pierced Ink
Madd Ink